Shut the Gate

Written by
Elizabeth Pulford

Illustrated by
Jenny Cooper

SCHOLASTIC
AUCKLAND SYDNEY NEW YORK LONDON TORONTO
MEXICO CITY NEW DELHI HONG KONG

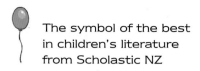

The symbol of the best
in children's literature
from Scholastic NZ

To my brother Michael and my sister Anna,
who were always part of the 'shut the gate' gang — E.P.

For Daniel and Logan, Timothy and Alex,
who always shut the gate! — J.C.

Published in 2006 by Scholastic New Zealand Limited
Private Bag 94407, Greenmount, Auckland 1730, New Zealand

Scholastic Australia Pty Limited
PO Box 579, Gosford, NSW 2250, Australia

Text © Elizabeth Pulford, 2006
Illustrations © Jenny Cooper, 2006

ISBN 978-1-86943-708-4

National Library of New Zealand Cataloguing-in-Publication Data

Pulford, Elizabeth, 1943-
Shut the gate / by Elizabeth Pulford ; illustrated by Jenny
Cooper.
ISBN 978-1-86943-708-4
(1. Walking—Fiction. 2. Domestic animals—Fiction.
3. Gates—Fiction.) I. Cooper, Jenny, 1961- II. Title.
NZ823.2—dc 22

9 8 7 6 5 4 3 2 1   6 7 8 9 / 0

Illustrations created using 2B pencil and watercolour

Publishing team: Christine Dale, Penny Scown and Annette Bisman
Typeset in Avant Garde 14/21pt by Book Design Limited, Christchurch, NZ

Printed in China

One bright spring morning,
Mum, baby Sara and Sam set off for a walk.

Out of the garden gate they went.

"Cluck-cluck," said the chickens.

"Cluck-cluck," said Sam.
"Da-da," said baby Sara.
"Shut the gate," said Mum.

And off they went,
into the grassy green paddock.

"Baa-baa," said the sheep.

"Baa-baa," said Sam.
"Da-da," said baby Sara.
"Shut the gate," said Mum.

Then out of the grassy green paddock
and into the muddy black field they went.

"Moo-moo," said the cows.

"Moo-moo," said Sam.
"Da-da," said baby Sara.
"Shut the gate," said Mum.

Out of the muddy black field they went,
on and on, up towards the rocky ridge.

"Neigh-neigh," said the horses.

"Neigh-neigh," said Sam.
"Da-da," said baby Sara.
"Shut the gate," said Mum.

At the top of the rocky ridge
they stopped for a rest.

"Cluck-cluck," said the chickens.
"Baa-baa," said the sheep.
"Moo-moo," said the cows.
"Neigh-neigh," said the horses.

"Uh-oh," said Sam.

"Da-da," said baby Sara.

"Who forgot to shut the gates?" asked Mum.

Then from the sky
came a tremendous, thunderous rumble.
Big black clouds began to gather.

"There's a storm coming," said Mum.
"Da-da," said baby Sara.
"Uh-oh," said Sam.

So down the rocky ridge they ran,
away from the coming storm.

"Faster!" cried Mum.
"Da-da," chuckled baby Sara.
"Shut the gate!" called Sam.

"Neigh-neigh," said the horses.

Through the muddy black field they ran,
away from the coming storm.

"Faster!" cried Mum.
"Da-da," chuckled baby Sara.
"Shut the gate!" called Sam.

"Moo-moo," said the cows.

Into the grassy green paddock they ran,
away from the coming storm.

"Faster!" cried Mum.
"Da-da," chuckled baby Sara.
"Shut the gate!" called Sam.

"Baa-baa," said the sheep.

Then through the garden gate they ran,
away from the coming storm.

"Faster!" cried Mum.
"Da-da," chuckled baby Sara.
"Shut the gate," said Sam.

"Cluck-cluck," said the chickens.

At last, into the house they ran,
as the first drops of rain fell.

"Just in time," said Mum.
"Da-da!" said baby Sara.
"Shut the door," said Sam.